MW01170059

Keep in touch!

Join my "Secret" Murder Mystery Lovers **Book Club!**
Get exclusives on new releases, Free-promotions, **contests** and **weekly** book giveaways!!
https://leadmagnets.leadpages.net/carol-durand/

Connect Facebook:
facebook.com/AuthorCarolDurand
Follow me on Twitter @AuthorCarolD
& on Pintrest @ CarolDurandAthor

Dedication:
To the boundlessness of life (the infinite) and love.

Table of Contents

Chapter 1

Melissa Gladstone inhaled the heavenly fragrance of her latest creations with a blissful smile. These cupcakes could very well be her best batch yet. She'd been experimenting with sweet and savory combinations and had come up with the ultimate breakfast cupcake, The French Toastie. There were decadent swirls of buttery cinnamon and brown sugar in the center, and crunchy bits of bacon dotted the maple-infused icing. The scent alone was certain to cause her loyal patrons to start queuing up early for the warm, fresh taste treats.

She heard the bell over the front door jangling, and, glancing at her watch, surmised that it must be her assistant Ben coming in. Ben was a grad student majoring in Criminal Justice who worked at Missy's Cupcakes and More for spending money. There were many times Melissa more than suspected that the poor boy was subsisting on day-old cupcakes, and would load up bags full of leftovers for him.

"Hey Ben, come back here," she called out from the kitchen, "you HAVE to try these!"

She nearly dropped a full pan of her breakfast concoctions when an unfamiliar deep, resonant male voice replied, "Ms. Gladstone, this is Detective Beckett from the LaChance police department, may I have a word with you?"

Setting down her tray and wiping her hands reflexively with a kitchen towel, Missy headed out of the kitchen, wondering. She couldn't fathom that a police department as small as LaChance's had actual detectives – nothing ever happened in this slow, sleepy Louisiana town.

"Good morning," she smiled tentatively, reaching out to shake the hand of the breathtakingly handsome man whose towering presence seemed somewhat out-of-place in the whimsical pink and lime-green interior of the cupcake shop. "We don't have any donuts, sorry," she giggled, her attempt at a joke falling awkwardly flat in the face of his intensely serious disposition. She was more than a bit intimidated by the steely blue gaze of Detective Beckett, and his seeming inability to smile was disconcerting to say the least.

"What can I help you with?" she asked, sobering and feeling the tiniest bit embarrassed at her potentially offensive remark.

Detective Beckett appraised her thoroughly, and despite having nothing to hide, she felt uncomfortably exposed beneath his penetrating gaze. Her enormous grey eyes widened and she unconsciously smoothed a curling tendril of bouncy blonde hair back from her brow when he finally spoke.

"I'd like to ask you some questions, Ms. Gladstone, it shouldn't take too long," he fixed her with his gaze and pulled a note pad out of his trench coat.

"Umm…certainly," she agreed, wondering. "Let's sit over there," she gestured to a small café table that was far enough away from the front counter and windows to ensure privacy. She didn't mind talking to the dashing, lantern-jawed detective, but she didn't necessarily want passersby to witness his presence. She hoped that the conversation would be brief, the shop opened in half an hour, and Ben wasn't scheduled until mid-morning, although he often came in early.

"Would you like some coffee, Detective? Or a cupcake? I have some fresh out of the oven," she offered, trying to make up for her earlier faux pas.

"No, thank you," he replied without changing expression. "Let's get started."

Missy was completely thrown off by the detective's remote manner. Her irreverent sense of humor, lighthearted personality and slight Southern drawl usually defrosted even the iciest of folks. In any case, her curiosity was piqued, wondering what could be so important as to render this man stoic in the face of her hospitality.

"Did something happen?" she asked, "Should I be worried? Is Ben okay?" She never had occasion to deal with the police other than attending their annual charity ball every year, and just realized that the fact that a detective came to her shop to speak to her could be an indication that something might be terribly wrong.

"Let's start there," Beckett replied, jotting down something on his notepad. "Who is Ben?" he asked, piercing her with his eyes. She tried not to fidget under his scrutiny. It had been quite a while since a man had made her squirm and she wasn't at all comfortable with the feeling.

"Ben is my assistant; he helps me with baking, running the shop and deliveries." The detective took a full report demanding Ben's full name, address, work schedule, school schedule and habits before returning to more pointed questioning.

"Where was Ben and what was he doing between the hours of 8 p.m. and 1 a.m. last night?" he asked, watching carefully for any reaction from Melissa.

"I have no idea," she replied, baffled. "I would guess that he was either in class or studying, that's how he spends most of his time – that boy is determined to make his way in this world," she assured him.

"So you'd say he's ambitious, willing to do whatever it takes to get ahead?" Beckett probed.

"Absolutely," Missy nodded vehemently, "I love that about him," she smiled broadly, clearly proud of her young assistant.

"Are you in a romantic relationship with Ben?" he quirked an eyebrow.

"Goodness no!" she exclaimed. "I'm almost old enough to be the boy's mama," she chuckled at the absurdity of the question. Truthfully, she had only turned 40 last month and thanks to a faithful gym and skin care regimen, she looked years younger, but her fondness for Ben was purely maternal.

After making some notes in handwriting that could only be described as chicken scratch, Detective Beckett snapped his notebook shut and tucked it back inside the flap of his coat. He handed Missy a business card with instructions to call him if she thought of any details regarding Ben or his whereabouts last night that might be of interest. Locking the door behind the detective – she'd really have to start being more diligent about keeping it locked when she was there alone in the morning – Missy pulled her cell phone out of the pocket of her stylish but practical jeans and dialed Ben's number.

Detective Chas Beckett drove away from Missy's Cupcakes and More deep in thought. His encounter with the owner, Melissa Gladstone had been entirely positive. If she was hiding something, she was a master of deception. The total lack of guile in those enormous kitten-grey eyes had him stumped. How could someone who was so close to the main person of interest in the Davis murder be entirely innocent? Still, he'd met his share of skilled liars in his time, and she just didn't fit the profile.

He had a full day ahead - now that he'd interviewed Ms. Gladstone, it was time to track down her seemingly squeaky-clean assistant for questioning. Depending upon how the conversation with Ben Radigan played out, he'd either be booking a suspect, or further investigating the crime scene evidence.

This one was going to be messy. Beckett had been called out in the middle of the night after one of the uniforms on patrol discovered that someone had left the lights on in the back room of Darryl's Donuts. When the officer went to investigate and found the rear entrance door ajar, he entered the sweet-smelling premises and nearly stumbled over the body of its owner, Darryl "The Donut Man" Davis slumped on the floor. Darryl was not sleeping, he was not unconscious, The Donut Man was dead, and still clutching a half-eaten chocolate crueller. Careful examination of the scene revealed no obvious cause of death – there were no signs of trauma, no tell-tale blood stains and no evidence that a struggle of any kind had occurred, yet Beckett was suspicious. He'd seen quite a few stiffs in his 22 years on the force, and something about this one wasn't quite right. He'd ordered a full forensics work-up, including a comprehensive search for trace evidence, fingerprints and an autopsy of The Donut Man, staying on the scene personally, observing the careful gathering of evidence, making sure that the crueller was taken gently from Davis' grasp and bagged as well, which made for a very long night.

The results of the autopsy would take a while to come back – the local coroner didn't have much in the way on his case list, but the testing and lab results could take a few weeks. Chas received a call from the lab while en route to interview Melissa and discovered that preliminary tests had come back on the half-eaten crueller and indicated that Darryl Davis had been poisoned. Further tests would be conducted, but the tech on the phone with Beckett speculated that it was common rat poisoning. The case had just leaped in classification from "Suspicious Cause of Death" to "Homicide."

Maybe he should've taken Melissa
Gladstone up on her offer of coffee and
a cupcake – he'd certainly had more
than a passing thought about how he
wished the two could've met under more
pleasant circumstances. The lovely,
curvaceous southern belle had definitely
piqued the interest of the somewhat
taciturn detective. He'd had to
consciously resist her charm and
hospitality in order to do his job
effectively. Having interviewed friends
and family members of Darryl the Donut
Man, Beckett discovered that there had
been some contention between the
portly, jovial fellow and Melissa
Gladstone over a prize-winning recipe.
According to those who should be in a
position to know, Darryl had somehow
obtained a cupcake recipe of Missy's
that he altered just slightly to make a

donut version and entered it into a national competition, winning a significant amount of money which allowed him to expand and advertise his business. Melissa, being a woman who believed in dignity (and the exacting repercussions of Karma), didn't pursue legal action against Darryl; but advised him never to speak to her or set foot in her establishment again. Finding it impossible to believe that this sweetly diminutive woman would exact any sort of physical vengeance upon her cross-town rival for the affections of the breakfast crowd, speculation naturally fell to Ms. Gladstone's fiercely loyal assistant, Ben. The boy had no family in town and didn't have much spare time to pursue friendships, so his ties with Melissa Gladstone were definitely significant. How significant remained to be seen. Sighing audibly and running a hand through his lush, jet black hair, Beckett turned his thoughts reluctantly away from the beautiful blonde and back to the tasks at hand. He pulled into the drive of the small rental home that Ben inhabited when not at work or school, and put his game face on.

"Ben!" Missy hissed into the phone, frightened, "What on earth is going on?"

"Huh?" Ben mumbled, confused. He had just woken up after a night of studying and couldn't fathom why his boss was calling him so early. "What do you mean? Am I late?" he yawned hugely.

"You need to come to the shop right now, we need to talk," she replied, urging him on, her voice clouded with worry.

Ben rubbed the sleep from his eyes, not comprehending the seriousness of Melissa's directive. "Mmmm...okay," he muttered sleepily. "I'll grab a quick shower and be right there," the clueless youth promised.

Missy sighed, frustrated, "Okay, but hurry Ben, please?"

His curly mop of mocha-colored hair still damp from the shower, Ben Radigan went about his morning routine with no more sense of urgency than if Melissa had never called. He figured that whatever it was that she needed to talk with him about could at least wait until he fed his cat, threw his laundry in the dryer and had his first two steaming mugs of coffee. After all, he reasoned, if it had been really important, she would've told him about it on the phone, right?

He took his aromatic cup of java to the dining nook and sat down to begin the process of waking up and starting his day. Surprised by the ringing of his doorbell, foliowed by an insistent pounding on the front door, Ben shambled to his small entryway and peered out the peep hole. Much to his surprise, his line of sight out of the peep hole was blocked by the shiny chrome of a police badge, and he quickly moved to open the door.

"Get your shoes Mr. Radigan, I'm bringing you in for questioning."

Chas Beckett tapped his pen against his desk blotter in consternation. Ben Radigan was no longer a suspect or even a person of interest in The Donut

Man murder. He had guilelessly given Beckett a detailed accounting of his whereabouts between the hours of 6:30 p.m. until 2:30 a.m. and had his story corroborated by two professors, a librarian and her assistant and six members of his study group. The kid really was as squeaky clean as he seemed – which left the detective the unpleasant task of considering who might have the motive to poison Darryl Davis. Reluctantly, he admitted to himself that he would have no choice but to question Melissa Gladstone again, she had just become a primary person of interest.

Melissa had heard of the demise of Darryl The Donut Man from one of her early morning regulars shortly after Detective Beckett had left. Caught up handling the morning rush by herself when Ben failed to appear, she didn't even have time to try to call her young assistant again until it was nearly lunchtime, and was dismayed when he didn't answer. She didn't believe for an instant that the dear boy had anything to do with the tragedy at Darryl's Donuts, and would fight tooth and nail to help prove his innocence if necessary.

Missy was turning the lock on the front door, preparing to head for home when, finally, Ben drove up in his time-worn little blue car.

"Ben!" she exclaimed with utter relief. "Thank goodness you're okay! Where have you been?" she demanded, worried.

They went back inside to catch up and Ben relayed the story of his experiences with Detective Beckett and the police department. Melissa was relieved to hear that he had been cleared of any wrongdoing, but still troubled by the fact that a scary tragedy had occurred in their quaint, cozy town. Locking the shop securely behind them, she and Ben went their separate ways, determined to put the unpleasant day well behind them.

The brisk Fall breeze and the thought of a dangerous person in town caused Missy to shiver involuntarily and she pulled the lapels of her light coat up around her neck protectively as she walked from her driveway to her front door, keys in hand. She lived in a lovely part of town that was quintessentially Southern, (right down to the massive magnolia tree in the yard), in a sprawling, turn-of-the-century Victorian that was a vibrant yellow with white trim. Her corner lot was bordered by an ornate wrought-iron fence that complimented the intricate scrollwork on the house itself. The house had been in rough shape when she first purchased it several years ago, but she lovingly restored every inch of the grand dame, and she knew every rustle, creek and sigh that the elegant lady made in protest of growing older.

The day had drained Melissa. Too tired to even think about preparing dinner just yet, she started water for a pot of tea and ran a warm bath in her oversized clawfoot tub. After tending to the needs of her exuberant Golden Retriever, Toffee, she sank gratefully into the bubbles of her bath, mug of tea in hand, eighties music on the stereo. Closing her eyes, basking in the relaxing warmth of the water, she turned the events of the day over and over in her weary mind. Why would someone have killed Darryl? He might not be the most scrupulous of people, but he certainly didn't deserve that! Who could've done such a heinous thing? And why on earth would anyone have suspected sweet, innocent Ben of such an act? Melissa was baffled and vowed to not think about it anymore, at least for tonight. Letting her mind drift peacefully to warm beaches and sunny days (her favorite mental vacation), she was startled out of her reverie by the loud, ferocious barking of the dog.

"That's strange," Missy mused aloud, "Toffee almost never barks." A chill went through her as she tried desperately to remember if she had locked the front door when she came in. What if whoever killed Darryl is targeting local business owners? What if she was next? "Calm down, be reasonable," she counseled herself, intentionally taking deep breaths in and out. "You have no idea what prompted that reaction from Toffee, just be calm," she tried to reason with her fears, with limited success. She quickly pulled the stopper, draining the water from the tub and silently slipped from the bathroom into her bedroom, pulling on the first warm clothes that she found. Hitting the button on the stereo remote, she turned off the music, listening intently as Toffee alternately barked savagely and whimpered.

"Hey darlin', what's got you so riled up, huh?" she cooed to the glossy Golden, whose hackles were raised as she stared fixedly out of the dining room window. When Toffee turned back briefly to glance at her, the whites of the agitated dog's eyes were showing, clearly indicating distress. Moving to the her gentle pet's side, Melissa peered out into the darkness, seeing nothing, hearing nothing but Toffee's low throaty growls.

"Well, Toffee girl, if someone's out there, maybe we should just go say hello, don't you think?" She received a brief swish of a feathery tail in response, but the dog refused to budge from the window. Grabbing a jacket and a flashlight, she snapped a leash on to Toffee's collar and headed for the door.

"Here goes nothing," Missy said grimly through teeth which chattered from a combination of cold and fear, "If we go down, we go down fighting, right girl?"

Switching on the flashlight after opening the front door, Melissa and Toffee headed down the steps of the verandah and around the left corner of the house, where the bay window in the dining room bumped out over the immaculate lawn. Toffee put her nose in the air, sniffing, straining at the leash, whimpering.

"I smell it too, girl…cigarette smoke," she observed, frowning. She let Toffee take the lead and the Golden practically dragged her immediately to the space outside the dining room window. The smell of smoke was even stronger the closer they got to the house. Missy shone the flashlight at the patch of grass below the window and saw a cigarette butt resting there. Taking a tissue from her pocket, scared and chilled to the bone, she carefully picked up the butt with the tissue and, folding the tissue around it, stuck it in her pocket. From the rear of the house, she heard what sounded like the crack of a brittle twig snapping, and Toffee's low growl became a roar. Terribly startled, Melissa twitched Toffee's leash to get her attention and ran for the front porch. Mounting the stairs two at a time with her faithful companion right at her heels, she charged into the house, locking the door behind her and securing the deadbolt. Shortly after slamming the front door, she heard the telltale screech of her cranky wrought-iron gate. Too terrified to even go the window to see who or what was leaving the yard, she crouched down and hugged Toffee tightly against her, burying her face in the reassuring warmth of her furry friend.

Chapter 2

"Thank you for seeing me, Detective Beckett," Melissa said in a hushed tone, taking a seat across the desk from him.

"I was actually planning to call you and ask you to come in, so you saved me the trouble," Chas replied politely.

"Glad I could help," she smiled despite her worries, as usual receiving no response or encouragement from the handsome investigator.

"Why don't you tell me what you'd like to say, then I'll have a few questions for you, sound fair?" he inclined his head, waiting for her agreement.

"Absolutely," Missy nodded vigorously, nervous to explore her strange encounter last night. She told him all about the dog barking, the smell of smoke, the creaking of the gate and gave him the cigarette butt that she had pocketed, and was astonished when he proposed very commonplace explanations for that particular series of events.

"No, Detective Beckett," she insisted vehemently, "my dog does not bark at squirrels, my gate does not come unlatched in the wind and none of my friends are smokers. There was someone lurking in the shadows around my house last night and I would really appreciate it if you'd help me get to the bottom of it!" Tenting his fingers beneath his chin, he studied her for a moment before replying.

"Exactly where were you on Monday evening between the hours of 8 p.m.

and 1 a.m.?" he asked, pursing his lips thoughtfully.

"I was at home, where I always...wait a minute, what does this have to do with anything that we've been discussing? I told you where I had been the night before when we spoke at the shop. And I don't see what that has to do with reporting an intruder," Missy finished, eyes narrowing.

"Don't you?" Detective Beckett questioned, leaning forward, so close that she could faintly smell his expensive cologne. "Doesn't it seem awfully convenient to you that "coincidentally" there's an intruder lurking around your house the night after your arch-rival is murdered across town?"

"That's exactly my point, I could be next on the list!"

"And who would have a motive to harm you?" Chas quirked an eyebrow.

"I have no idea. Who would have motive to harm Darryl Davis?" she asked, firing back. He looked at her pointedly from across the desk, and she suddenly realized why he had wanted to talk with her today.

"You think I did this???" she demanded in a stage whisper, verging on tears. "How dare you?" she accused. "Darryl Davis and I had our differences to be sure, but I would never wish something like this on anyone! I don't even know how he died, the paper didn't say." Her lower lip trembled and she crossed her arms across her chest, furious at Beckett's rude insinuation.

The detective sat back in his chair, staring at her thoughtfully and sighed.

"You're not being accused of anything at this time, we are merely treating you as a person of interest in this case due to the nature of your relationship with Mr. Davis," he spoke in the least reassuring tone she'd ever heard. "Don't leave town, even to go shopping, without letting me know where you're going and why – we may need to ask you more questions."

"Why on earth would I leave town? I have a business to run," Missy was incredulous. "And let me tell you something Detective Beckett," her grey eyes turned steely, "I have worked hard my entire life for all that I have, and I find your attempt to sully my reputation with your ridiculous accusations offensive to the extreme!" She stood, shaking slightly with the force of her indignation and dug in her purse for her keys.

"Noted," he sighed, never taking his eyes off of her.

Beckett frowned after Melissa Gladstone stormed from the room. On paper, she was the obvious choice for primary suspect, but his gut told him that all was not as it seemed. He couldn't put his finger on it, but something was telling him that suspecting Cupcake Missy of a crime was seriously barking up the wrong tree. He still believed that there was most likely an innocuous explanation for the previous evening's events, but decided to take the cigarette butt to the lab, just in case it turned up something interesting. He hated the thought that the feisty blonde might actually be in danger, so it only made sense to follow up on her story.

"No rush," Chas told the bored lab tech at the evidence window, "check for fingerprints, DNA, chem, locators, the usual."

Missy fumed all the way back to the store. How dare that arrogant icicle of a human being accuse her of committing a crime? Clearly, the police had no credible leads and were looking at her as an easy target. Well, she'd show them and show them good – if they were too incompetent to find Darryl Davis' killer, she'd have to do it herself. Ben was a Criminal Justice major – surely he'd have some good advice for her.

"Stay out of it Ms. Gladstone," Ben warned, shaking his head. "The police know what they're doing and are trained to handle this kind of thing. Seriously, what are you going to do if you come face to face with a killer?" he raised his eyebrows at her.

"The police know what they're doing? Are you kidding? The police think I did this! I have to prove them wrong, I'm not going to sit idly by while they ruin my life with false accusations," she insisted stubbornly. "And I have no intention of coming face to face with a killer, I'm just going to figure out who did it and turn them in."

Ben was nonplussed. "It's really not that simple Ms. G," he frowned, concerned.

"Sure it is honey," she patted his arm. "I have the truth on my side, and the truth shall set me free, just you watch!" she nodded, determined.

Ben caved under pressure when he realized just how determined Melissa was to seek out Darryl Davis' killer.

"Ok Ms. G.," he began, talking around a mouthful of delicious Morning Glory cupcake, "the first thing you should think about is: who would do this and why? You need to figure out if the Donut Man had any enemies or bad debts, did drugs or engaged in any kind of risky behavior that would drive someone to murder. Lots of times the best place to start is by figuring out whether he was in a relationship or had an angry ex-wife or something," the young man advised, washing down his mouthful of cupcake with a swig of coffee. "Wow, these are amazing today, what did you do differently?" Ben asked, holding up the last bite of his cupcake.

"I used dates along with raisins, it keeps them more moist," she murmured absently, taking notes on Ben's instructions. She left her sidekick to his cupcake and moved to the computer to do some research – looking for any info that she could find on Darryl the Donut Man Davis.

"Ben, c'mere and look at this!" Missy ordered excitedly from the back office at the cupcake shop.

"Hang on Ms. G., I'm just finishing up closing and then I'll be back there," he called while putting chairs upside down on top of the tables.

She looked at her watch surprised at how the time had flown. She'd been poring over local archives and articles for hours and finally found something that might be worth pursuing. Ben was puzzled when she pointed to a picture of 5 people holding trophies on a stage.

"What's this all about?" he queried, confused.

"This is a picture of all of the winners of the contest that Darryl entered when he pirated my recipe and used it to make donuts."

"Okay, so why is it significant?"

"Look at the guy standing on Darryl's left – can you make out the look on his face?" she pointed to the screen.

"He doesn't exactly look happy," Ben observed.

"Of course he doesn't," Missy crowed triumphantly, "He came in second! If Darryl hadn't stolen my recipe, he would have won."

"But does he know that?" the youth asked, wanting to proceed cautiously and not jump to conclusions.

"I know for a fact that he does, because he and another contestant who was later disqualified for hygiene reasons overheard me when I confronted Darryl about it," she finished, folding her arms to underscore her point.

"Wow. Well, that does seem like it's worth looking into, just try not to get too excited until we have our facts lined up, okay?" he cautioned.

Chapter 3

"You want motive? Check out this motive," Melissa smugly tossed a copy of the photo that she had found online onto Detective Beckett's desk, along with several articles detailing the checkered past of the 2nd place winner, Giacomo Andretti, who was rumored to have ties with organized crime.

Chas raised a skeptical eyebrow at her, glanced at the pile of paper in front of him and advised, "You might want to have a seat and lower your voice, Ms. Gladstone."

"Why would I want to do that? I'm working for the best interests of the general public – that's something to be proud of," she challenged, chin jutting out defiantly. Beckett stood to his full height then placed his hands on the desk, leaning toward where Missy stood, hands on hips tapping her foot. "From where a lot of these folks are sitting, it looks very much like you are working for your own best interests by trying to point the finger at someone else," he said quietly. "Now for my part of things, I don't believe you're guilty of anything other than being slightly paranoid and having issues with authority figures," he almost smiled, "but you can help me to help you by sitting down and showing me what you've come up with." He locked eyes with her, then looked pointedly at the chair beside his desk. Chagrined, she sat, folding her hands in her lap.

She explained her findings to the detective, who became very attentive when she told him that Andretti had witnessed her argument with the Donut Man.

"I'll check it out," he promised, clearly impressed that she had done her homework. "Don't get your hopes up, chances are he had nothing to do with this, but I'll have a little chat with him and see where things go from there."

Missy extended her hand, grateful to have seen at least a shred of human compassion in this tough cookie. "Thank you so much Detective, I really appreciate this," she smiled and gripped his warm, iron-strong hand, butterflies fluttering madly in her midsection. She mused that it was truly a shame that this magnificent male never demonstrated any personality traits aside from impeccable professionalism.

Chas Beckett was mildly shocked by the tenderhearted reactions that this vivacious woman inspired in him. He'd never show it of course, he'd perfected the appearance of disinterested impartiality over the years, but his encounters with Melissa Gladstone rekindled an awareness of feeling in him that he would prefer remained buried for eternity. His life was straightforward, uncomplicated - he had no wife, no kids, no pets, nothing other than a fantastic wardrobe, a modest house and car and a job that consumed every waking thought. Just the way he liked it. Until recently, that is. More than once, his thoughts had touched upon the endearing qualities possessed by the tiny but tough blonde, qualities that had begun to tear at the corners of the impenetrable fortress that he had built around his heart years ago. Shaking off this dangerous train of thought, he focused on the task at hand and reached for the phone.

Beckett's conversation with Andretti left him suspicious, but unconvinced. His gut told him that there were likely many things of which the baker was guilty, but as to whether or not the murder of the Donut Man was one of them was still a matter requiring further investigation. He received a phone call from an anxious Missy Gladstone that evening and reassured her that he would be looking into the matter further. He hung up the phone feeling a bit sad and very much aware of his singular status. His simple cottage was sparsely decorated in neutral tones and, while peaceful, was not exactly what one would classify as a cozy retreat from the outside world. He spent most of his time at home sitting at the desk in his home office, working on cases, puzzling over clues and looking for resolutions to loose ends. He worked out at the gym every day and jogged when the weather permitted it, but rarely indulged in personal time aside from those pursuits. He was smart enough to know that he was a shell of a man, empty inside, but trying to make a difference in the world, and he was mostly okay with that.

Melissa found herself trying to think of creative excuses to meet with the dashing detective more often, but refused to examine her feelings in the matter. She had been just fine on her own (thank you very much!) for years now, and the thought of allowing another person into her world was somewhat preposterous, particularly considering that the person in question was a human iceberg. She went through the rest of her week on automatic pilot, just going through the motions of daily life, while waiting to receive some semblance of hope from Detective Beckett.

Chapter 4

 By Saturday morning, she couldn't stand the suspense any longer and decided to take matters into her own hands. Stepping out of her burgundy cube car in front of Bodacious Bakery, Giacomo Andretti's somewhat dingy but well-known sweet shop that had thrived for years in a much larger town roughly 45 miles from LaChance, Melissa took a deep breath to steady her nerves and headed for the entrance. The teenager working behind the counter was quite friendly as she pretended to study the selection of cakes and pastries while surreptitiously glancing about, looking for something (anything!) that looked suspicious.

"I'm sorry, sweetie," she cooed in her most motherly voice, "do y'all happen to have a ladies room?" She knew from having been in the bakery years ago that there were no public facilities.

The teenager leaned over the counter conspiratorially and said in a low voice, "I'm not supposed to do this, but I can let you use the employee rest room if you promise not to tell my boss."

"My lips are sealed, darlin," she beamed at him as he pointed, directing her to go down the hall and turn left. She went down the hall and turned right instead, heading for the kitchen. Entering the stainless steel commercial space, she quickly scanned shelves looking for clues of any kind. Bingo! There it was…sitting on a shelf below one of the massive commercial sinks was a large box of rat poison. How they were able to pass health inspections under those sorts of conditions is a mystery probably best explained by the plethora of friends in low places that Andretti had acquired over the years.

One of Ben's fellow grad students worked part time at the mortuary, assisting with embalming and preparations of the deceased. He had discovered in some carelessly stored paperwork that the deceased, one Darryl Davis, had been poisoned and that the tentative identification of the substance causing death was thought to be rat poisoning. And right here, right now, in Giacomo Andretti's kitchen, she had discovered a big box of the stuff.

Taking her phone out of her purse in order to take a photo, Missy froze when she heard a raspy voice with a heavy Italian accent say, "And what is it that a

beautiful lady is doing in my kitchen?"
The words were friendly, but the voice
had menacing overtones. Melissa's
heart pounded in her chest as she
whirled to face the large Italian man.
She plastered a wide smile on her face,
fighting madly to keep her voice from
shaking.

"Oh my goodness, I'm so sorry – I
wandered back here looking for the
ladies' room, am I going the right
direction?" she feigned innocence,
hoping that her performance was
convincing.

"We don't have a ladies' room, but I'd be
happy to escort you to my employee
restroom if you'd like," he offered, too
smoothly.

Missy was not about to allow this man to
escort her anywhere, but she once

again worked up some sugar and spice, hoping to get out of there alive.

"You know what, I think I'll just wait, I'm headed straight home after this anyhow," she crinkled her nose flirtatiously, pulling out all the stops.

"You look very familiar to me…" the dark Italian observed, narrowing his eyes. "Have we met?"

She avoided the question deftly. "You know, people say that to me all the time – I guess I just have one of those faces." She beamed at him one more time and moved toward the door which led to the front of the store, fingers crossed that he wouldn't block her passage as she made her exit and got back in her car to head to see Chas.

Chapter 5

"Do you realize I could have you arrested for impeding an investigation?" Chas hissed at her, livid.

"How can you be upset with me when I found evidence linking him to the crime?" Missy shot back, hurt.

"Evidence? You call a box of rat poison evidence? There's probably one of those in every kitchen in Louisiana," he commented dryly, bursting her bubble. "And what made you think that rat poison is what killed Davis anyway?" he scorched her with his gaze.

"I'm not revealing my sources, but I have it on good authority that rat poison is what killed Darryl, and the fact of the matter is that someone who has motive to kill him is in possession of a great deal of it!" she stomped her foot in frustration. "Can't you just arrest him for something and then do a search to see if you find anything?" she pleaded.

Beckett sighed, running a hand through his hair, exasperated. "No, we can't just arrest him, there has to be a reasonable suspicion of guilt and there are proper procedures involved." He came around to the side of the desk where Melissa sat fidgeting in her chair. "Look," he said quietly, "I told you that I would look into it, and I am looking into it, you need to trust that I've been following up on every possible lead." He held her gaze and part of her melted at the concern that she saw in his eyes. For the first time in a long time, she was at a loss for words. It had been a long, tiring week and suddenly she felt entirely drained.

"When's the last time you had a decent meal?" Beckett suddenly asked almost sternly.

Thinking about it, Missy realized that she hadn't eaten since dinner yesterday and her stomach growled audibly in response. She giggled, embarrassed by the expression of her hunger and admitted that it had been almost 24 hours.

"I'll meet you in an hour," he shocked her by saying. "We'll continue this discussion at the steak house if that works for you. I could use a good meal myself," and he actually allowed the corners of his mouth to lift briefly in a gentle and devastating smile.

Missy's insides shook like well-made aspic whenever she thought about her impending meal with the handsome

Detective Beckett. She changed her blouse three times, finally settling on a bright blue silk that looked perfect with the ivory trousers that she had selected for the occasion. She brushed out her gleaming cornsilk tresses, leaving her hair falling gently down around her shoulders in a glorious cloud of soft curls, and finished her look with a touch of eyeliner and lip gloss. Simple sapphire studs adorned her ears and she admired their sparkle in the mirror. Missy knew that she was probably putting way too much thought into the evening, Beckett probably just wanted to pick her brain for more ideas about the case, but she was an old-school Southern woman and when a gorgeous man asked her for the pleasure of her company, she would dress for the occasion, no matter what his motives might be.

Toffee followed her from room to room as she prepared for her evening (she refused to call it a date, she hadn't been on one of those for a couple of years), the tags on her collar jingling as she moved. Missy had watched her carefully after the incident with the cigarette butt and the creaking gate, relying upon the retriever's keen sense of hearing for clues to any possible intruders, but the mellow Golden hadn't seemed to notice anything unusual in the last couple of days. She bent down to ruffle the fur on the top of her beloved friend's head.

"Well Toffee Girl, it may not be a date, but I'm going to enjoy the heck out of sitting across from Detective Chas

Beckett this evening," she grinned happily at her pet, surprised at the butterflies that fluttered lightly in her midsection.

After pulling his third choice of shirt impatiently over his head and throwing it on his bed, Chas frowned at his own behavior. Why was he making such a big deal over something as simple as two hungry people sharing a meal together? It wasn't like it was a date or anything, he reminded himself. After his fiancée had left him at the altar all those years ago, he had vowed that he would never allow another woman to get close enough to him to devastate his soul the way that Chloe had. Until now it hadn't been an issue, although many willing and able young ladies had practically thrown themselves at his feet over the years, he had managed to keep them at arm's length until they realized that he meant what he said when he declared that he was married to his work and that she was a jealous wife. Sighing, he pulled a deep purple button-down from its velvet-clad hanger (organization was a priority in his life and his closet highlighted the concept), and pulled it on. The shirt was perfect, but looked far too upscale for the perfectly fitted dark-wash jeans that graced his hips, so he grabbed a pair of charcoal-colored woolen trousers that completed his look. He glanced at his watch, ran his fingers through his hair, smoothing it into place, hurriedly fastened his favorite watch to his wrist, grabbed a coordinating sport coat and headed for the door. He was never late. His father had been a military man who insisted upon impeccable manners, which included pathological punctuality, and the practice of arriving never less than ten minutes early had served Beckett well. He was always prepared, always ready for whatever awaited him, and always in control of himself and his surroundings, so why on earth was there a somewhat breathless sense of anticipation coursing through his veins at the thought of sitting across the table from the lovely Melissa Gladstone? It had been a long week and he hadn't eaten in quite a while – he was quite certain that once his belly was full, he'd return to his normal state of detachment. At least that's what he told himself.

Missy arrived at the Happy Horseshoe Steak House, trying not to notice how her heart leapt into her throat when she saw Detective Beckett's low-slung sport sedan already parked in the lot. Breathing deeply to steady her inexplicable bout of nerves, she took one last glance in her visor mirror, fluffing her curls with her fingertips before heading toward the restaurant. Her breath caught yet again when she saw him sitting alone in a candlelit booth, seemingly perfectly at home against the rich soft leather of the seat. His casually elegant appearance made her heart beat faster than it had in quite some time and her smile was anything but forced as she approached the table.

Beckett stood and lightly touched her arm to guide her to her seat and Missy had to work hard at suppressing a shiver of excitement at the feel of his touch through the light silk fabric. She sat across the table from him, uncharacteristically at a loss for words, still intimidated by his even gaze.

"I took the liberty of ordering a wine that is a delicious complement to the steaks that are featured," he began. "I hope you don't mind," he raised an inquiring eyebrow. Missy wondered absently if he had any idea how devastatingly handsome he looked when he used that expression.

"Not at all," she murmured, smiling shyly. "A good pairing makes all the difference!" she exclaimed, mortified the moment the words left her mouth and hoping that he didn't take them the wrong way. "I mean, with wine and food, you know…they're really much more tasty when paired correctly," she babbled, blushing. Much to her surprise and delight, a slow grin spread across Beckett's finely chiseled features and he nodded.

"I couldn't agree more," he came to her rescue. "The right wine and food pairings can be extraordinary." Missy returned his smile, relieved and was more than glad to see the approach of the waiter, bottle of wine in hand.

"Detective Beckett, I can't tell you how grateful I am for the work that you're doing on the case," Missy said, earnestly, sipping the delightful Cabernet that he had selected for the occasion.

Beckett held up a hand to interrupt her. "First, please call me Chas; and secondly, let's not talk about the case right now. I think we could both use a break from it for at least the duration of our meal," he gave her a pointed look, but softened it with a slight smile.

"I think you're absolutely right, Detect – I mean, Chas," she agreed, loving the sound of his name on her lips. "And please, call me Missy," she directed.

"It suits you, Missy," he tipped his wine glass toward her and she clinked hers lightly with his. "Tell me about yourself," he invited after appreciating his sip.

"I'm afraid there's not much to tell," she admitted ruefully. "I was born and raised in this tiny town. I've done some traveling, but not nearly as much as I'd like, and the shop takes up practically every second of my time," she shrugged.

"I know the feeling," Chas nodded. "Do you have any family in town?"

Missy eyed him speculatively. "Is that a personal question or a professional one?" she challenged lightly.

She was treated to another flash of that devastating smile. "Personal, no business tonight, I promise," he asserted, hands up in mock self-defense.

"No, no family," she dropped her gaze, but not before he noted the touch of melancholy in her soft grey eyes. "My parents died in an accident when I was 17, leaving me with the family business. Friends and generous folks from the community helped me out with it until I graduated from high school, then I went to college part-time to earn my degree while I ran the store during the day. My younger sister helped out when she could, but she was in school too, so she could only do a few hours here or there." Missy quieted, caught up in her memories of the past, then shook her head as if to escape them. "Needless to say, it was challenging for a while, but I managed," she tried to smile.

"Wow, caring for a younger sibling while going to school and running a shop is pretty amazing for an adult, it must've been tremendously difficult for a teenager," Chas frowned sympathetically. He noticed that she smiled brightly, falsely, and changed the subject immediately when he expressed sympathy. He totally understood. Pain, anger and raw courage he could deal with – compassion and sympathy, not so much. He wondered how much more he had in common with this charming Southern belle.

"It all seems like a hundred years ago," Missy smiled, trying desperately for nonchalance. "What about you – do you have any family?" she inquired, more than ready to shift the focus of the conversation.

"My mother passed a couple of years ago, and my father is alive…physically at least. He's in a nursing home in upstate New York – I see him every couple of months, but on most visits he doesn't even know who I am," Chas showed a surprising vulnerability when he spoke of his father, Missy's heart went out to him.

"Oh Chas, I'm so sorry," she said softly. "Has he been that way for very long?"

"Too long," was the somewhat husky reply. "He would never have wanted to live this way," he finished gruffly. Missy started to reach for his hand, but held back when the waiter approached with their steaks.

"That smells fantastic," Chas noted, grateful for the interruption. Missy's stomach growled loudly in agreement and they both laughed, their shared moment dissipating into safer realms.

They shared the rest of their time together talking about current events (other than the Davis case), places they'd like to visit someday, and embarrassing childhood experiences that had them at times practically doubled over with laughter. It was, without exception, the best evening that either of them had experienced in a very long time, their carefree laughter drawing smiles and indulgent glances from their fellow diners.

Chas insisted upon walking Missy to her car, and, in light of recent events, (along with the fact that she was as pleased as a blushing schoolgirl at the prospect), she agreed.

"I had a really lovely time tonight," she smiled softly up at him, eyes shining. "Thank you so much – it was nice to feel like a person again," impulsively she lightly touched his arm, truly grateful for his company. He studied her for what seemed like a long time, smiling warmly. Her heart beat faster and faster. She gazed at the tempting fullness of his lower lip, wondering if he was going to kiss her. He noticed the focus of her attention and drew in a deep breath, seeming to come to some sort of decision.

"The pleasure was all mine," he said, clearly meaning it. He brushed his fingers gently over the hand that she had placed on his arm and stepped back, clearly reluctant to maintain distance, but needing to do so.

They said their respective goodbyes and Missy practically floated up her front steps when she got home, smiling dreamily and totally unaware of a presence in the shadows watching, waiting.

Chapter 6

Missy absently brushed the flour from her hands on the front of her apron before putting another batch of her popular Chocolate Cream Cheese Cupcakes in the oven. She had been working extra quickly this morning, trying to get everything in the kitchen done well in advance of her 7 a.m. opening time. Ben had called in sick – a first for him, he hadn't had a sick day the entire time he worked for her – and her heart went out to him, he sounded positively miserable. Which left her with all of the opening and customer service responsibilities, it was going to be a long day.

Humming to herself as she worked, Missy jumped a mile when she heard a familiar raspy Italian voice directly behind her. "You should be more careful about locking the door behind you," Andretti snarled in a menacing tone.

Heart racing, she whirled to face him, eyes wide with fear. "What are you doing here?" she demanded, her voice a tad shrill.

"You didn't admit who you were when you were snooping around in my shop last week," Andretti's eyes narrowed accusingly. "And I didn't remember you until the police came and started asking me questions," he continued in a low growl. "People who go looking for trouble usually find it. You'd do well to remember that, lady," he spat contemptuously, turning Missy's fear to ire.

"Is that a threat, Mr. Andretti?" she challenged, hands on hips, eyes flashing. Andretti took a deliberate step toward her, thrusting his face so close she could smell traces of last night's garlic on his hot, chuffing, breath. Missy stumbled away reflexively, fearing that the irate Italian would become violent.

"That," he began, enunciating and emphasizing every word with unspoken but nearly tangible malice, "That. Was. Not. A. Threat, little Missy." He stabbed his finger in her direction repeatedly, trembling in his anger, causing her to step back yet again. She knew this kitchen like the back of her hand and knew that he had her backed into a corner with no escape. For better or worse, when it came time for fight or flight, Missy's usual reaction was to stand up for herself. She may be in a bad position, but she'd be damned if she'd go down without a fight.

Inwardly loathing the weak-sounding tremor in her voice, she drew herself up to every inch of her diminutive height, thrust her chin forward with bravado that she almost felt, and declared, "Mr. Andretti, I think you'd better leave now." She was determined to stand her ground, come what may. She refused to cower before a bully, even if it killed her, and she was actually afraid that it just might.

"I'll leave when I choose," he thundered in response, his color rising, turning from red to nearly purple in his ill-contained rage. He moved in close to shout in her face again, but this time she refused to retreat, despite her revulsion at the hot stench of his breath and the spittle that launched forth. "Just you remember what I said, and keep that fragile nose of yours where it belongs – I'd hate to see something happen to it," he hissed through his teeth, turned on his heel and strode toward the back door. Grabbing a dishcloth before touching the doorknob, he spun to face her with a pointed glare that spoke volumes. He pointed at her, jabbing his finger toward her again, raised his eyebrows in warning, and backed out the door.

Missy heaved a giant sigh of relief, and ran trembling to lock the door after Andretti departed. She leaned back against it, willing her heartbeat to slow, taking deep breaths. An acrid smell teased her nostrils and she looked toward the ovens in alarm. Her cupcakes were burning and tendrils of smoke were starting to rise up through the burners. Furious, she raced over to turn off the ovens and decided against opening the shop today. With the burned disaster in the ovens she wouldn't have enough stock to make it through anyway, so she made a sign for the door and grabbed her car keys. Maybe Chas Beckett would believe her suspicions about Giacomo Andretti now.

Chapter 7

Rhonda Davis Burns sat across the conference table from Detective Beckett smoking a cigarette and distractedly tapping her ragged nails on the scarred and pocked surface while studiously avoiding his steely gaze.

"Did your brother have any girlfriends or ex-girlfriends with whom he had some sort of conflict?" he probed, impatient with Darryl's sister's reluctance to participate in the conversation. He thought that he had interviewed every living relative of the Donut Man, to no avail, and then Rhonda sauntered into his office at the insistence of her other siblings. She looked as though she had been pretty once, a long, hard lifetime ago. She stated her age as 28, but looked as though she was at least a decade older than that, with harsh lines around her mouth, deep frown lines on her brow and teeth and nails showing the dull yellow of neglect, and years of chemical experimentation.

"He kinda gave up on having a girlfriend after that Gladstone snob humiliated him," Rhonda drawled, taking a deep drag. Beckett wasn't sure he had heard her correctly.

"Gladstone?" he inquired, his pen poised above his notebook.

She snorted derisively, "You mean no one told you about her? That smug little babe ruined Darryl for good," she sneered. "He didn't date much before he tried to date her, but he didn't date at all once she destroyed what few shreds of manhood he had left." Chas put down his pen, needing to clarify what he thought he was hearing.

"Who are you talking about here?" he drilled her with a look.

"I told you, the Gladstone chick," she allowed a curl of smoke to drift from the corner of her mouth.

"Melissa Gladstone?" he offered, hoping that he was wrong.

"Oh hell no, Darryl knew better than to even try with that snooty little goody two-shoes, he went for the little sister, Sherilyn. He thought he was in love with that girl and she wouldn't give him the time of day. He asked her out quite a few times and she always turned him down. He sent her flowers and found them in the trash behind the cupcake shop. The last straw was when he bought space on the light board at the ballpark and asked her out between innings, in front of the entire crowd. She refused him, again, told him to leave her alone or she'd go to the police, and ran from the park crying. He tried calling her for a few months and used to ride by her house in his car, but he finally gave up. A few months later, she was dead," Darryl's sister shrugged as if her story was common knowledge, and of little consequence.

Beckett's mind was reeling. Why hadn't Missy told him about her sister and Darryl Davis? She'd had the perfect opportunity at dinner, and had changed the subject instead. And how did Sherilyn die? Unfortunately, he'd have to table these new questions until his interview with Darryl's sister was complete. He grilled her further, but received no information of any value, and finally sent her on her way, spraying a disinfectant room freshener after her departure.

Chapter 8

Missy quickly got out of her car, looking furtively about her to make certain that she wasn't followed, and trotted quickly up the cement steps to the LaChance police department to fill Chas Beckett in on her encounter with Giacomo Andretti. She checked in with the clerk and made her way to Beckett's desk. When he glanced up and saw her, instead of the welcoming smile that she expected, she was greeted with an icy glare.

"Chas?" she approached hesitantly.

"What can I do for you Ms. Gladstone?" he responded curtly, raising a skeptical eyebrow.

Missy was taken aback, they had parted on such good terms, and now it seemed that their lovely evening together had never happened. She had come to him today hoping for support and reassurance and was apparently going to receive neither.

"Umm…I really need to talk to you, it's important," she said quietly, puzzled at his behavior toward her.

"Well, isn't that a coincidence," he retorted sarcastically. "I have some things that I need to speak with you about as well, have a seat," he indicated to the worn leather chair across from him.

"Is something wrong?" Missy asked, worried.

"You haven't exactly been forthcoming with me in regard to your relationship to Darryl Davis have you?" Beckett got straight to the point.

"Of course I have," Missy sputtered, confused. "I have no idea what you're talking about, I've told you everything I know!"

"Everything?" the detective queried. "You want to rethink that?" he looked at her pointedly.

"Rethink what? I'm sorry Detective, I don't understand what's going on here, do you want to tell me what this is about, or are you just going to continue to vaguely accuse me of something and leave me in the dark?" she challenged.

Beckett sighed and leaned back in his chair, putting his hands behind his head, never taking his eyes from hers.

"Why didn't you tell me about Sherilyn?" he asked quietly.

Missy dropped her gaze, shoulders slumping. "I did tell you about her, there was nothing more to say," she offered lamely. Her words sounded hollow even in her own ears.

"Really?" he threw out sardonically. "You didn't think the fact that Darryl Davis essentially stalked your sister might turn out to be somewhat relevant to this case?"

"How could it be? My sister has been deceased for years," her eyes filled with tears as the wounds that she'd tried so hard to keep closed reopened, the pain as fresh as if it happened yesterday. Her sister was all she had left in the world and one day she was just…gone. Forever.

"And that was another detail that you neglected to mention. Your sister died under suspicious circumstances, a suspect was never named and I'm supposed to believe that it never crossed your mind that Darryl Davis should have been named as at least a person of interest in the case?"

Missy shook her head vehemently. "You know very well that there was no love lost between me and Darryl Davis, but as much as I disliked him as a business rival, he was never anything but sweet to Sherilyn. I don't believe for a second that he had anything to do with her death. The police eventually reported that it was accidental, and I've lived every day since believing that. No, Darryl may have been unscrupulous in business, but he didn't kill my little Sheri." She twisted her hands in her lap, biting down on her lip to keep from breaking down in front of the man whom she had come to admire, who was now looking at her as though her words were not to be trusted.

Beckett ran a hand through his hair, frustrated. Once again, his gut told him that Missy was innocent of any wrongdoing, despite what seemed to be a pretty damning omission in her statement, but he had no other prime suspects and the case was growing colder by the day. He'd be putting in some late hours this week, but then, that was the norm for him. His pleasant interlude with Missy at the steakhouse had been a mistake. For a moment he had allowed his personal feelings to cloud his judgment – that wouldn't be the case from now on. He would be strictly businesslike with this beautiful blonde person of interest.

"You said that you had something important to talk about," he said somewhat wearily, picking up his pen.

Chapter 9

Missy drove home in a daze, her thoughts far away. She hadn't thought about the details of Sheri's death in years. The reality of it was just too painful. Her sister had died of head injuries that appeared as though they were deliberate, but in the end were ruled as being accidental because no good explanation could be found as to how she suffered them. Her sister Sherilyn was a quiet, bookish girl who laughed easily and was a friend to everyone. The only reason that Darryl Davis thought he had a chance with her was because she was as kind to him as she was to everyone else and he read more meaning into her polite smiles and conversation than he should have. That he was bewitched by her lovely face and pleasant manner was no surprise, she had more than her share of wanna-be suitors, but preferred to spend most of her time alone with her music and her books, lost in world of her own where parents don't die prematurely, sisters don't take on the role of parenting, and life is simple and beautiful. The thought of hurting anyone caused Sheri great distress and she grieved for young Darryl Davis, knowing that her refusals were causing him pain, but unable to become involved in a close relationship with anyone aside from her beloved older sis.

Missy's melancholy clung to her like a dark cloud, and she trudged to the mailbox in front of her house not even noticing that the letter flap had been left open. Finding it empty, she made her way up the front steps, eager to bury her face in the silky fur of her loyal friend. When she stepped into the foyer, she immediately knew that something was wrong, her senses becoming instantly aware of several things simultaneously.

Toffee had an accident in the front hall, as evidenced by a large pool of urine, and the happy animal who typically greeted her at the door, was nowhere to be seen. There was a faint smell in the air that she recognized…fear. Animals put out a definitive odor when they are in a state of fear or distress and Toffee was no exception.

Heart in her throat, Missy called out softly, "Toffee? Where are you, girl? Toffee?" She was just beginning to panic when she heard a soft whine from the kitchen, and ran to see what had happened. Toffee was huddled in the corner, under a table, peering out warily, trembling. Her tail thumped twice when Missy held out her hand to the frightened animal, beckoning her to come out. The terrified retriever belly-crawled out to Missy, laying her tawny head in her lap.

"What is it, girl? Why are you so scared?" Missy cooed to her faithful friend, frightened herself.

The dog sat up and looked at her owner, then at the back door, then at her owner and back at the door again. Missy followed the dog's gaze and her breath caught in her throat – the door was ajar. She never left the house without locking both the front and back doors, particularly now that there was potentially a madman on the loose. She was rooted in place, not knowing whether or not to move quickly to lock the back door, or whether there might still be someone in the house. Fearing for her safety and Toffee's, Missy sprang into action, tiptoeing across the kitchen to grab Toffee's leash, then snapping it on the still-trembling animal's collar and practically sprinting out the front door with her. Locking herself and the traumatized animal safely in her car, she dialed Chas' number with shaking fingers.

Missy stayed in the car attempting to soothe Toffee, while keeping a lid on her own rising panic and waited for Chas and two more patrol cars to show up. She had kept her eyes glued on the house, and from her vantage point, had seen no one leave through either the front or the back door, which meant that either they were long gone before she arrived, or they were still inside the house. Chas and the four patrol officers approached the house, hands on their weapons, but not drawing any attention to the residence from curious neighbors, per Missy's request. Two officers stayed outside to secure a perimeter around the house, while Chas and the other two went inside, where they stayed for what seemed to Missy to be forever.

Chas approached her car to give her an update. "We dusted the doorknob for prints, but whoever touched it last wiped it clean." Immediately Missy thought of how Giacomo Andretti had grabbed a kitchen towel before exiting out the back door of the cupcake shop after their encounter, and mentioned the parallel to the detective. He responded that they would check it out, and that after exploring every nook and cranny of her sizable residence, they had found no evidence of an intruder, aside from some potato chip crumbs on the table in the kitchen. Missy had given up eating potato chips several decades ago and told him so. Nodding thoughtfully, Chas let her know that they had taken the crumbs as evidence and that he would let her know what they found out. Missy made the spontaneous decision that she would be traveling to another city this evening to stay in a hotel and Chas accompanied her into the house while she cleaned up the evidence of Toffee's accident, packed a light bag and some basic supplies for her beloved pet. Beckett was stationing a patrol car in the area, where they could observe the residence without being detected, and assured her that he would call if anything happened, counseling her to relax and get a good night's sleep. At this rate, she didn't know if she'd ever sleep again.

Chapter 10

Ben looked at his boss with consternation. There were dark circles under her eyes, and she clung to her coffee mug as though her life depended upon it, staring vacantly into space.

"Hey Ms. G.," the concerned young man began. "If you want to take a few hours to go home and sleep or something, I can handle things here," he offered, somewhat alarmed when she didn't respond.

"Ms. G.?" he prompted, a bit louder this time, causing Missy to come out of her reverie a bit.

"I'm sorry Ben," she ran a weary hand over her forehead. "Did you say something?"

He had never seen her so exhausted. His boss was a woman of action, when something was bothering her, she figured out a way to solve the problem, that's just who she was. Seeing her like this was making him gravely concerned for her health and well-being.

"I just...I said that I think you should go home and sleep and I'll take care of things here," he urged. Missy smiled at her kind-hearted assistant.

"Thanks for the offer Ben, but I'm not having much luck sleeping at home lately. Ever since I found out that someone had been in there, I've felt...I don't know...watched...violated. My personal space was invaded. They scared my baby girl," her voice broke a bit when she thought about how scared Toffee had been.

"Well, I understand how that could happen, but…isn't there someone who would let you crash on their couch for a bit or something?" he tried desperately to think of solutions that would help this poor, suffering woman.

"It's okay, Ben, really. It doesn't matter where I am or who I'm with these days, I'm not going to be able to rest until I get some answers. Someone is trying to send me a message and eventually we'll find out what it all means," she sighed, dropping her head down on her arms in exhaustion. "I really feel safest when I'm here," she mumbled. Ben awkwardly patted her on the arm in his innocent attempt to comfort her, and heard her snore softly.

"Well, at least she'll finally be getting some sleep," he remarked to himself, going back to his tasks.

Chapter 11

"What do you mean Andretti is in the clear?" Missy demanded, sitting in the uncomfortable leather chair across from Chas Beckett.

"He has airtight alibis for both events. There's no way he could have been at Darryl's on the night of his murder or at your house on the night of the break-in," Chas asserted gently. "He provided video evidence."

"But…how? Was it authenticated? If it wasn't Andretti, who on earth was in my house, and who killed Darryl? It just doesn't make sense," Missy shook her head in dismay.

"Yes, the videos were authenticated, it's a dead end, we need to find someone else with the motive to do what they did, assuming that the two events are even related," he mused.

"Of course they're related," she insisted. "There's no way that Darryl's death and someone suddenly stalking me could be a coincidence. Oh Chas, what am I going to do?" Missy lowered her face into her hands, finally giving in to the tears that had been threatening since the whole horrible mess had begun.

Beckett observed her, torn. One part of him thought that it would be all too easy for her to try to throw him off her trail by distracting him with supposed break-ins, but the other part of him, the way-down-deep-inside part of him that was rarely (if ever) wrong, felt that she was as much of a victim as Darryl was, although not quite as finally…yet. But he was frustrated by the lack of leads and evidence in the case. He vowed to leave no stone unturned until it was solved, and if that meant having to convict the sweet, lovely woman who sat sobbing in front of him, so be it.

Missy was frustrated, with herself for breaking down in front of anyone, but particularly Chas Beckett, and with her situation. She couldn't understand why it was taking so long for the police to find Darryl Davis' killer, and she had an eerie feeling that she just might be the next victim. She hated going home these days, there was a pervasive chill in the stately house that had nothing to do with the thermostat setting. Toffee seemed to have recovered entirely from her strange encounter with an intruder, but Missy noted that the animal seemed more vigilant than usual, pacing up and down in front of the windows and sometimes fixating on particular spots in the darkness beyond. As a precaution, she had disposed of the dog's food and replaced it with new – she couldn't bear the thought that someone just might be evil enough to try to poison her furry friend. She changed the locks on all of her doors, had expensive deadbolts installed, and put guard bars in her windows.

 Yet, even with all of the precautions, she still jumped at every sound, investigated every shadow, and hardly slept at all. Her fears were taking a toll on her health. Her face was pale, with deep shadows under her eyes that no amount of concealer could hide, so she didn't even bother to try, and she hadn't been able to force herself to eat an entire meal since the incident. She nibbled delicately and scraped the majority of her meals into the garbage disposal. Weight loss made her look a bit gaunt, and her clothes were starting to hang loosely.

She could have taken the sleeping pills that dear Doc Wiley had provided when she complained about her insomnia, but the nagging fear that something would happen that would require her to have her wits about her, prevented her from seeking pharmaceutical relief.

Knowing that she desperately needed some rest, she made herself a cup of chamomile tea, just like her grandmother used to make, while she ran a bath with lavender crystals that the woman at the health food store assured her were supposed to induce sleep. At this point she was willing to try anything to get some rest. Her teakettle whistled merrily, and the happy sound took her back to simpler days. Pouring the steaming water into her cup to brew, she wished that life had taken a different path. She missed her parents and her sister still. Time had eased the pain, but certainly hadn't eliminated it. She wondered if staying single all these years so that she could focus on keeping the family business alive had been a mistake. Going through recent events would have been much easier with someone strong, capable and loving by her side.

Chas Beckett's handsome face popped into her mind and she forcibly dismissed the thought of him. She thought they had shared a special time together, and had enjoyed seeing the softer, more personable side of the taciturn detective, but now he looked at her as a possible murderer. How on earth could he believe something like that after spending time getting to know her? Well, it's not like it mattered anyway, he wasn't looking for a relationship and neither was she. Going solo might be lonely, but the intricacies and difficulties of relationships could be more painful than the pangs of loneliness, so she had probably been right to avoid the whole emotional mess – it was safer, in a manner of speaking.

Shaking herself from her reverie, she dunked her teabag up and down several times, squeezed it out and headed for the bathroom with Toffee at her heels. She waited until the adoring canine settled herself on the bathmat in front of the sink, then locked the two of them in. She wasn't letting the dog out of her sight whenever she was home, just as a precaution.

She sank back into the delicately scented warmth of the bath and drew in a deep breath. The water felt wonderful, and she felt some of her stress melting away. Missy sipped her tea, savoring the familiar taste of home and family, then tipped her head back and closed her eyes, relaxing a bit. She was luxuriating in the feeling of finally being warm and somewhat sleepy when her cell phone buzzed from its spot on the countertop. Sighing, Missy decided not to jump up from her watery retreat to run across the cold porcelain floor to answer it. Whatever it was could wait, she reasoned, and if it was important, the caller could leave a message. She was exhausted and refused to deal with anything (or anyone) else for the rest of the day. Lingering in her bath for nearly half an hour (and adding hot water periodically to keep it soothing and warm), Missy noted that the chamomile tea and lavender crystals seemed to be having their intended effect, as her eyes drooped heavily. Rising slowly out of the healing waters, she padded over to the towel bar and wrapped the large, fluffy bath blanket around herself. She glanced at her phone and saw that Ben was the mystery caller, and that he had indeed left a message. She yawned hugely and decided to listen to his voicemail tomorrow. Sleep was fast approaching and she was going to take full advantage of the opportunity.

Drying off and slipping into thick, pink flannel pajamas, Missy headed down the hall and gratefully cocooned herself in the pillowy depths of her fluffy down comforter, drifting off into the first heavy sleep she'd had in a very long time. Toffee snored softly from her plush doggie bed in the corner of the room, and all was peaceful for the rest of the night.

Chapter 12

Missy awoke with a start, dismayed to
see sunlight streaming through the
windows. She had to have overslept, at
this time of year she was always up and
baking before sunrise. She felt guilty,
particularly because she knew that Ben
would already be hard at work, waiting
for her to come in. She took a quick
shower, dried her hair in such a hurry
that curly tufts sprang up in every
direction, causing her to toss it on top of
her head in a loose bun to contain it,
and threw on the first sweater and clean
pair of jeans that she could find. She
brushed her teeth, grabbed her coat and
keys and flew out the door, pausing only
long enough to let Toffee come trotting
out behind her. Once the dog was done
with her morning relief, Missy let her

back in the house, locked the door securely behind her and headed for her car.

The shop was dark when its harried owner arrived, causing her to wonder what was going on. Ben was nowhere to be found, and Missy remembered that he had left her a voicemail last night. Hurriedly punching her code into her phone, after a brief pause she heard Ben's voice. He sounded as though he had a cold.

"Uh, hi Ms. G.," he began haltingly. She heard him take a deep, shuddering breath. "I'm really sorry, but I might not be able to open the shop tomorrow," his voice cracked with emotion and Missy's heart dropped at the thought of what might be making him so upset. "When I, umm…came home tonight," the clearly distraught youth choked out, "Rocky was really sick, so I took him to the vet…and they…they don't know if he's…" Ben's voice cut out, he was overwhelmed. Missy had never heard him so upset. Another shuddering breath. "Anyhow, they'll know more tomorrow…so…I'll call or something. I'm really sorry." Click. The message ended. Missy's heart went out to the youth, and she hung up her phone sadly. It never rained but it poured, poor Ben. It was rough making it through the business day without her loyal assistant, but she understood how he felt. He was alone in the world and Rocky was his best friend. If something happened to the gentle cat, Ben wouldn't get over it easily.

So many times during the day, Missy reached for her phone to call, but she knew that Ben would update her when he knew something, and customers kept her busy pretty consistently, giving her little time to think about his awful circumstances. She had just turned off the bright neon pink "We're Open" sign and locked the front door to the shop when her phone rang. Seeing Ben's number on her screen, she answered immediately.

"Ben, sweetheart, are you okay? How's Rocky?" she asked tenderly, before he even had a chance to speak. When a small sound like a soft sob was his reply, she knew right away that the worst had happened.

"Oh Ben, I'm so sorry, what can I do? What do you need? Have you eaten?"

Missy went into nurturing mode, like she used to when Sherilyn used to cry for their parents in the night. Wishing she could give him a hug, she listened as he recounted the events of the evening before, his tears fading into faint hiccups.

Ben was perplexed when Rocky didn't greet him at the door by twining between his legs as was his custom. Their routine was like clockwork – he would pick up the snuggly feline and scratch him behind the ears, then it was time to go to the kitchen where he'd pour kibble into Rocky's bowl. Rocky would wait patiently for Ben's dinner to come out of the microwave (or for the pizza delivery man to arrive) and then when Ben sat down to eat, Rocky would attack his food like the mini-lion that he pretended to be. The two would eat in companionable silence, then retire to the living room for TV. It was more than strange that Rocky broke from routine, and Ben went through the house calling his name.

He found the poor cat curled up on his side, on top of a heat register, in the corner of the bedroom, mewling miserably. His eyes were glazed and had a pained expression and the poor animal had white foam drizzling from the corners of his mouth. Ben gingerly picked him up and his dear friend felt almost rigid in his arms. He wrapped him in a blanket and drove him to the emergency veterinary hospital, where the doctor took one look and spirited the miserable cat to an examination room immediately. He told Ben that, at first glance, it looked as though Rocky had gotten into something poisonous, but that it would take some testing to be sure. In the meantime, they were going to keep Rocky overnight to give him fluids and keep him under observation, but the prognosis didn't look good. At 4:30 a.m., Ben received a call requesting that he come in as soon as possible. Rocky wasn't going to make it and breathed his last gasping breath cradled gently in the arms of his owner, while tears flowed freely down the stricken youth's face.

Ben had wrapped Rocky carefully in the blanket that he'd brought him to the vet in, and took him home, where he buried him under the winter-barren branches of a rose bush in a corner of the back yard. With no one around to hear or see, the grief-stricken young man leaned pitifully on the handle of his shovel sobbing with all his might.

When Missy heard the terrible tale, her heart broke for Ben and she cried with him over the phone. She reassured him that he could take as much time as he needed for his grief, but he insisted on coming in the next day, knowing that work would help take his mind off of the incredibly untimely loss of his furry friend. She hung up the phone after murmuring words of comfort that most likely fell upon deaf ears, and wrapped her arms around her waist, aching with sorrow. She didn't know if she could take another tragedy and hoped desperately that something good would happen, and soon.

Chapter 13

Nearly a week had passed since Missy had medicated herself with chamomile and lavender, and she hadn't had a good night's sleep since. Being an animal lover herself, the news of Ben's beloved cat, Rocky, dying had rocked her world. He seemed to be coping well, but who knew what pain he experienced every time he walked in his door. Once again desperate for a good night's rest, as much as she loathed the idea, Missy took one of the sleeping pills that she had been prescribed, feeling that she wouldn't make it through the work day tomorrow after yet another sleepless night.

She was dreaming. It was a balmy summer evening and she was at the carnival. Brightly colored lights flashed around and around as the Ferris wheel took her higher and higher, then swooped toward the ground. She could hear the drumbeats of a band but not the music. The drumbeats got louder and louder, drowning out every other sound. Suddenly, someone was shouting above the staccato drumbeats, calling her name, beckoning her down from the Ferris wheel. There was danger. She needed to get off the Ferris wheel and couldn't open the safety lock. She panicked.

Sitting bolt upright in her bed, panting with fear, Missy saw the bright blue and red flashing lights of a squad car painting the walls of her bedroom in frightening rhythm. There was pounding at her front door and a deep male voice was calling out to her.

"Ms. Gladstone? Ms. Gladstone, are you in there? Ms. Gladstone, can you hear me? This is Officer O'Leary, can you open the door Ms. Gladstone?" More pounding.

Terrified, Missy snatched up her thick baby blue bathrobe, throwing it on over her pajamas, and slid her feet into her slippers, dashing out into the hall. She ran to the front door, nearly tripping over Toffee, who was cowering in the foyer, the fur on her scruff standing straight up. She opened the door to see Officer O'Leary standing on her front porch.

"Are you all right ma'am?" he asked, concern coloring his words as he did a quick assessment of her physical state.

"Yes, I'm fine, why? What's happening?" she asked in alarm.

"May I come in?" he inquired, peering past her, into the house.

"Of course, please. Where are my manners?" she murmured, bewildered.

"No worries, ma'am, I'm sure you're understandably startled," he followed her into the foyer, eyes darting methodically to every corner of the room.

"What's going on?" Missy asked, genuinely worried, noting the policeman's vigilant behavior.

"Mrs. Fielding, your next door neighbor, called us to report an intruder at your residence. She saw someone near your bay window." Missy's hands flew to her mouth in horror. "When our unmarked patrol car arrived on the scene, the intruder fled down the alley behind the

Fielding's, into the woods on the other side of the railroad tracks, and out of sight."

"So you didn't catch him?" the terrified woman whimpered.

"No ma'am, I'm sorry, we didn't," the officer admitted ruefully. "We have a team outside, looking for clues, so we'll be here a while."

"I understand. Can I get you anything? Coffee?" the southern hostess in her took over automatically.

"No thank you, ma'am. We'll just get what we need and be on our way. The detective will be here in a few minutes to ask you some questions, and I'd like to check out your security systems and the rest of the house right quick if you don't mind."

"No, please, go ahead – do whatever you need to do," Missy replied, still stunned by the night's events and desperately trying to shake off the numbing effects of the sleeping pill that she had taken. She heard another knock at the door and went to answer it while O'Leary inspected the house. Standing on her doorstep, looking somewhat chagrined and quite serious, was Detective Beckett.

"Hi Missy," he said softly. "May I come in?"

"Of course, Detective," she returned coolly, turning around and heading for the kitchen table. She pulled out a chair for herself and sat, indicating the chair across from her for Beckett. The look on her face spoke volumes, as she arched an "I told you so" eyebrow at him.

"Look, I'm sorry I dismissed your concerns earlier. I promise you, we are going to make every effort to find out who was trespassing here tonight and bring them in for questioning," he assured her earnestly.

"Well, at least you believe me now," she pointed out shakily, glad to finally be vindicated, at least in this regard.

"Did you see or hear anything tonight?" Chas probed gently, noting that Missy was still shaking like a leaf. She shook her head vehemently.

"No. Unfortunately, I was so exhausted tonight that I actually followed the doctor's orders and took a sleeping pill so that I could finally sleep. The first thing I heard was Officer O'Leary pounding at the door," she confessed, miserably.

"Sorry about that," Beckett apologized. "In cases like this, the first thing that we do is make certain that the resident is safe and sound."

"No apologies," Missy dropped her head into her hands. "I was more than relieved to see a policeman at my door rather than a boogeyman."

Chas gazed sympathetically at the understandably overwrought woman and made his questioning brief, reassuring her that his team was thoroughly combing the grounds and surrounding area for any hint of a clue.

"Do you have somewhere to stay tonight?" the detective seemed genuinely concerned.

Missy shrugged, "No. Where would I go in the middle of the night? I have no idea what to do," her lower lip trembled as tears threatened.

Beckett took a deep breath. Seeming to come to a decision he offered, "I have a completely unused guest room if you'd like to stay somewhere safe for the night."

Knowing that she was completely safe under Chas Beckett's roof for the night, Missy made sure that Toffee was settled into her puffy grey velour doggy bed in the corner of the guest room and, after

an hour or so of tossing and turning,
finally dropped into a deep sleep.

Chapter 14

She awoke in the morning, rested, but
still very unsettled. As diligently as the
handsome detective had been in trying
to find new leads and exhaust every
possible avenue for information, nothing
constructive had been found. Not being
one to sit around and let fate take its
course, Missy vowed to get to the
bottom of this case, her life might very
well depend upon it, but before she
could begin ferreting out elusive clues
that would help solve the case, she had
to open the shop. Ben had his annual
physical this morning, so Missy's
sleuthing would have to wait until he
came in at 11:00.

Business was booming this morning,
and Missy hardly had a spare moment
to even think until the rush ended

around 10:30. She had restocked the gleaming glass cases with delectable treats and was wiping down the tables which had recently been cleared, when she heard the tinkle of the chimes above the door. Expecting to see Ben coming in early, she turned and saw a harried-looking woman who appeared a bit younger than her, stride briskly over to the counter.

"Hi! I'll be with you in just a..." Missy began, only to be interrupted by the impatient woman.

"I'd like a Strawberry Cheesecake cupcake, to go," she ordered brusquely. Missy was nonplussed. Most of her customers were completely willing to take their time placing an order, chat for a bit, and maybe even sit down for a cup of coffee.

"Certainly," she agreed politely, wiping her hands on a towel behind the counter and slipping on a pair of plastic gloves. "Can I get you a cup of coffee with that?" she offered. "I can make it…"

"No coffee," the woman interrupted again, frowning.

"…to go," Missy finished, frustrated, but pasting what she hoped was a sufficiently pleasant smile on her face.

Missy reached into the case, selecting the largest, most luscious looking Strawberry Cheesecake cupcake and placed it in a bag for the rude woman.

"That'll be $3.50," she said with forced cheer, handing the woman the bag.

"Keep the change," the woman decreed abruptly, slapping four bills on the counter and rushing out the door.

"Thank you," Missy called after her. "Have a nice day," her voice dripped with sarcasm after the woman was long gone. She shook her head and went back to wiping down the tables and thought about her plan for the afternoon, leaving as soon as Ben came in.

Darryl Davis' mother played bridge with Missy's parent's years ago, so Missy felt that she could drop in on the elderly woman without the fear of being rebuffed. It was a long shot, but Widow Davis might just know something useful. She parked in front of Mrs. Davis' small but elegant cottage with its neatly manicured lawn and lovingly tended flower beds that were so well kept they looked presentable even despite the winter chill.

Holding her breath and desperately hoping that the woman was still of sound mind and would recognize her, Missy rang the bell, hearing a lovely chime within the house when she did. Listening intently, she heard stirrings that sounded like Mrs. Davis might be shuffling toward the door. Sure enough, she opened it and smiled with delight at the sight of a visitor.

"Well…Missy Gladstone, as I live and breathe!" she exclaimed with a grin. "Come on in, dear, I haven't seen you in years, we have some catching up to do," she beckoned Missy in with a gnarled but graceful hand.

"Thank you Mrs. Davis, it has been a long time, hasn't it?" Missy agreed, taking in the lovely antiques, polished floors and fine fabrics decorating the cottage.

Leading Missy to a velvet wingback chair in the parlor, Mrs. Davis made her way to the kitchen and came back with a tray laden with tea, cream, sugar and a plate of homemade sugar cookies. Taking a cookie to be polite, and finding it utterly delicious, Missy indulged Darryl's mother with lighthearted conversation about her work and how she had been, receiving a wealth of stories in return, related to Mrs. Davis' bridge-playing exploits, who was seeing whom in her church congregation, and the current state of her garden. After nearly an hour, Missy felt that she could almost comfortably broach the subject of Darryl's death, her actual reason for visiting with the widow.

"You must miss Darryl terribly," Missy observed sympathetically.

A faraway look descended over the widow's gentle face. "Oh I definitely do," she agreed softly. "There were some things that we disagreed upon, but he was a good boy, my Darryl. He made some mistakes in this life, to be sure," she gazed sadly at Missy, "but deep down, where it counts, he was a good boy."

"I'm sure he was, Mrs. Davis, I'm sure he was," she patted the widow's hand reassuringly. "Who's running his shop now?" she asked with a "just-curious" expression.

"His brother David," she replied, seemingly lost in memories. "So many folks have come by the store to express their sympathies at his passing. It brings me comfort to know that he was so loved," she smiled faintly. "There's even someone who anonymously drops off a hydrangea blossom on the back stoop at his house every morning." Missy's ears perked up at this tidbit…it could mean something. "They were his favorite flowers you know, hydrangeas. The blue ones, specifically." Widow Davis suddenly looked very tired and was beginning to ramble a bit, so Missy took her leave, eager to gather more information that might help Detective Beckett find the horrible person who killed Darryl. If she could help crack the case, she just might find out who had been lurking about outside her home and avoid being the next victim. She had a hunch to follow and drove with determination to her next stop.

There was no one in Darryl's Donuts when Missy entered the sweet-smelling shop, save for the fresh-faced teenaged girl behind the counter.

"Hey, Ms. Gladstone!" Darryl's niece, Debbie, sang out.

"Hi Debbie," she replied with a smile. "How have you been?"

"Pretty good," the bubbly girl responded. "I mean, you know, it's been kinda tough around here without Uncle Darryl and all, but we're doing okay I guess," she shrugged, determined to hold on to optimism.

"I bet," Missy sympathized. "Your Grandmama told me that folks have been coming by to talk to y'all about what a good man he was."

Debbie nodded vigorously. "Yep, there's one lady who has stopped in here every morning for a really long time, and she still comes in every day. I think of her as "Strawberry Cheesecake," because she gets our Strawberry Cream Cheese Danish every day at 7:20 – it never fails. Well, almost never, I didn't see her this morning," the teenager mused, as a lightbulb suddenly snapped on within Missy's mind.

Strawberry Cheesecake??? The rude woman who stopped into her shop this morning ordered a Strawberry Cheesecake cupcake – was it possible that she had killed Darryl and was now setting her sights on Missy? Missy had to find out more about this mystery woman – she just might be the key to cracking Darryl Davis' murder. After all, doing the same thing every morning for years at a time…wasn't that a bit pathological? Of course, people have habits, but Strawberry Cheesecake's habit was unhealthy and seemed…obsessive. Missy's fevered brain tried to wrap itself around this new revelation while still appearing to focus on the chattering girl behind the counter. She made mindless conversation for a few more minutes, just to be polite and not seem suspicious, but she was anxious to get away in order to think through her next move. She needed to find out more about Strawberry Cheesecake. Should she investigate on her own? Should she call in Detective Beckett? It seemed to her that every lead that she turned over to the detective led to a dead end, so maybe she should arm herself with more information before alerting him to a potential new suspect. Missy had never even considered the fact that the killer could be a woman. Had Darryl made a nuisance of himself with Strawberry Cheesecake the way that he had with Missy's beloved little sister? Or worse? And if that were the case, why would the woman have anything against Missy? She needed to think, so she headed home to make a cup of tea, grab a snack and form her plan of attack. The fact that a woman who was known for ordering the same thing every morning from Darryl and that a rude woman came into Missy's shop and ordered a cupcake version of the same thing, could be just a coincidence, but with the strange events of late, Missy wasn't taking anything at face value. "Strange coincidences" seemed to be the norm these days, and she was going to chase down every possible clue.

Sitting in the sunny nook of her kitchen's eating area with Toffee curled up at her feet, Missy sipped at her tea, nibbled at her small bowl of pretzel crisps and pondered the events of the day. Darryl's mother had mentioned that someone was leaving a single hydrangea blossom on his stoop every morning. Perhaps that person would have had a close enough relationship to Darryl to know something about who might have the motive to kill him. All she would have to do is hide away somewhere near Darryl's house, and when the mystery visitor came to drop off the flower, Missy could start a sympathetic conversation that could lead to more clues. Never having been involved in any sort of intrigue, she had no idea about the potentially dangerous situation that she could be putting herself in. It seemed that the Cheesecake lady might provide more relevant info than the mysterious flower giver, because her behavior seemed more bold, so Missy vowed to be parked near Darryl's Donuts by 7:20 tomorrow morning in order to follow her to see what information could be unearthed. For now, she would make notes regarding her findings in a notebook that she had been using to keep track of information that seemed relevant. Quickly jotting down dates, times and "facts", she didn't notice the passing of time, and was surprised when she at last looked up, to see that the sun had begun its descent and the air had cooled rapidly. Drawing on a sweater to combat the chill, Missy was startled when her phone rang.

"Ms. Gladstone?" Detective Beckett's serious tone was inescapable. "I need to speak with you…now. I'll be at your door in ten minutes, we need to talk."

Missy's heart beat fast, wondering if the detective had finally found out something crucial to cracking the case. Chas was somber and frowning when she opened the door to admit him.

"Have you found something?" Missy asked breathlessly, leading him to the kitchen table to have a seat.

"I've found enough to make a difficult case seem even more difficult," he sighed, running a frustrated hand through his hair, ruffling the thick locks in a tousled manner that made him even more attractive, Missy noted. He glanced over at the notebook that she had been keeping and leaned closer to glance at the pages, so she discreetly closed the cover and put her mug of tea on top of it, using it as a coaster.

"Would you like some tea?" she asked, trying to divert his attention.

"No, I'm fine thanks," he responded, getting down to business. "Do you wear lipstick, Ms. Gladstone?" Missy was baffled.

"On special occasions," she replied, mystified. "I'm more of a lip balm gal – it's much more practical…why?"

"Could you please bring me any tubes of lipstick currently in your possession?" his request sounded much more like an order. Taken aback, Missy opened her purse and extracted a tube, then told the detective that she'd be right back. As she emerged from her bedroom carrying two additional tubes, Chas was examining the first lipstick and making notes in his ever-present flip-pad. He took the next two tubes from her and did the same.

"Mind if I borrow these for a couple of days?" he asked, pulling a small plastic bag out of his trench coat pocket.

"Of course not," Missy consented immediately. "But why on earth do you want my lipstick?"

Ignoring her question, Beckett demanded to know if she had any other tubes. When she told him no, he stood to go.

"Are you going to tell me what's going on here?" she demanded, beginning to get upset at his reticence.

"Just following up on some leads," he said dismissively. "I'll let you know if we find anything significant." He strode toward the door, ending the conversation. Missy was entirely befuddled.

"Wait!" she called out, stopping him in his tracks. He turned slowly to face her. She wasn't going to give him an inkling about the Cheesecake lady, she was following up on that one on her own. But perhaps she could be more efficient by having him track down the mystery hydrangea giver.

"Darryl's mother told me something today that might be important," she said urgently, walking toward where he stood unmoving by the door.

He quirked a disapproving eyebrow at her. "And why, exactly, were you speaking to Mr. Davis' mother?" he demanded, his displeasure evident.

"She was a friend of my parents," Missy hedged, crossing her arms over her chest defiantly. "Don't you want to hear what she said?" she challenged.

"Fine," Beckett sighed. "What did she say?" he reached into his pocket, bringing out the flip-pad. Missy related her conversation with Widow Davis, leaving her other activities of the day deliberately absent. Chas took notes here and there, then snapped the flip-pad shut, fixing Missy with a piercing gaze.

"Stay away from this, Ms. Gladstone," he warned soberly. "You aren't making your circumstances any better by interfering with my investigation," he admonished.

"My circumstances?" she exclaimed. "This has nothing to do with my circumstances," she asserted. "I'm just trying to help you find Darryl's killer," she frowned, bothered by the detectives detached demeanor.

"Respectfully, Ms. Gladstone…when I want your help, I'll ask for it," Chas assured her wryly, opening the door, exiting and closing it firmly behind him. Missy mechanically went through the motions of locking the door knob and securing the deadbolts. She didn't know what was wrong with Chas Beckett, and why he was treating her as an enemy rather than an ally, particularly in light of the lovely dinner they had shared, but she was determined to move forward in her plan to gather more information that might just help find a killer.

Chapter 15

Adrenalin, along with a not-inconsiderable amount of caffeine, made Missy's heart race as she prepared for her first stake-out. She wanted to look as inconspicuous as possible, so she dressed more casually than she typically would during a workday, donning comfy yoga pants, a thick sweatshirt and running shoes. She didn't know what she might encounter, so it made sense to be comfortable. There was a thin crust of frost on her windshield, which was unusual this time of year in Louisiana, and, because she didn't own an ice-scraper, she tidied the frosty windshield with a spatula, the cold air seeping right through the thin fabric of her yoga pants. Shivering a bit, she cranked the heater in the pre-dawn morning and headed for Darryl's Donuts. It took her a few minutes to find a vantage point from where she could watch the shop, unobserved. She parked the car and turned off the engine, snugging her hand-knitted scarf tighter around her neck, determined to follow Strawberry Cheesecake wherever she might lead. Missy had arrived at 7:15, not wanting to miss the obsessed patron, and was soon rewarded as she saw the angry woman from the cupcake shop get out of a sleek maroon sports car in front of Darryl's Donuts. Her heart pounded as she held her breath, waiting for the woman to emerge from the shop. Fortunately, she didn't have to wait long, catching sight of the woman heading back to her car, coffee in one hand, a small bag in the other. Missy waited just long enough to be unobtrusive, before starting the car and pulling into the lane behind the woman at a safe distance.

Strawberry Cheesecake had a tendency to exceed the speed limit, making it a challenge for Missy to keep up, but keep up she did. The Cheesecake lady pulled into an alley, parking behind the Fleur de Lis flower shop. Missy parked down the street, just far enough where she could see without being seen, and watched carefully as the woman pulled keys from her purse and unlocked the door to the flower shop. So apparently, the surly woman with a penchant for pastry was the proprietor of the Fleur de Lis. Thinking fast, Missy turned off the car, and after waiting for 15 minutes or so to allow the woman to get settled into her morning routine, she got out of the car, heading for the flower shop. Small bells above the door tinkled merrily as Missy was engulfed in the glorious scent of multitudes of domestic and exotic blossoms. It smelled like paradise and she was almost distracted from her task, but was sharply reminded when the woman behind the counter spoke.

"Oh my, you've found me," she lamented, shocking Missy profoundly. This woman remembered her? Could it be because she had been watching, stalking or terrorizing her? "Listen, I'm so sorry," she continued, "I know I was positively rude when I came into your store yesterday. My blood sugar was low, I was running late and didn't have enough time to stop at the place where I typically get breakfast, and my behavior was inexcusable – I'm so sorry. I'm not normally like that," she assured Missy contritely.

Missy faked a giggle. "Oh, that's okay, I see people before they get their morning coffee all the time, it's not a pretty sight." She couldn't help but wonder if this woman had been the person lurking around her house at night. A realization exploded into her brain and she devised a tactic to test a new theory that had just occurred to her. "I actually didn't "find" you at all," she reassured the harried woman. "I happened to be in the neighborhood and I need an arrangement of flowers for my niece – she's in the hospital," Missy lied smoothly, desperately hoping that this woman didn't know that she had no niece. She really was not skilled in subterfuge and was internally kicking herself for blurting out something that could easily be discovered as a lie.

"Oh, I'm sorry," the woman responded with ersatz sympathy. "Is she going to be okay?" she inquired politely.

"She'll be fine," Missy continued to lie. "I just wanted to brighten her day."

"What a lovely sentiment," the cold woman smiled, feigning interest. "What sort of arrangement would you like?"

"Well," Missy began, swallowing a bit convulsively. There was no turning back now. She might be tipping her hand, but she had to get to the bottom of this.

"Her favorite color is blue, what would you suggest?" she asked, trying to sound innocent.

Flowers were clearly the remote woman's joy in life, her face lit up at Missy's question, as she pondered the wealth of possibilities.

"Well, we have some lovely irises that are a bluish-purple, and we could put some white roses in for an elegant touch, and fill out the rest of the arrangement with hydrangeas, I have a new shipment in that is the most beautiful blue you've ever seen!" she finished enthusiastically. Bingo. That was the information that Missy was looking for.

"You have hydrangeas? I just love hydrangeas! I think the arrangement sounds perfect, when can I pick it up?" Missy asked, excited at the realization that her ruse had worked. She had just put together that Strawberry

Cheesecake and the flower giver might just be the same person.

"Absolutely," the woman gushed, "my shop is the only one in the area that carries hydrangeas. I'll have my assistant, Andrew, start on your arrangement as soon as he gets in and it should be ready for pick-up around noon, sound good?"

"Perfect," Missy responded slyly, pleased with herself and exhilarated to think that she might have made a breakthrough in the case. She paid in advance, with cash, for the arrangement that she had no intention of picking up, not wanting this woman to have any of her information. It dawned on Missy that her life might be in danger now more than ever, but she was determined to proceed. Besides, if Strawberry

Cheesecake knew that Missy was suspicious, it might make her more cautious, buying her and Detective Beckett more time to solve the case. She knew that she should be sharing her findings with the now entirely-professional, and clearly romantically-uninterested detective, but she wasn't ready just yet, she had one more stake-out to conduct.

Missy left the shop and went through the rest of her day in somewhat of a haze, focused exclusively upon the resolution that her plan for the next day might bring. She felt absolutely certain that, one way or another, the truth would be revealed, sooner rather than later, and if she was the only one with the tenacity to see it through, so be it.

Sitting at the vanity, brushing her blonde curls carefully while mulling over the day's events, Missy was utterly lost in thought when her phone buzzed insistently. Startled from her reverie, she snatched up the noisy instrument and answered it immediately when she saw Ben's number on the screen.

"Hi Ben!" she sang out cheerfully; always glad to hear from her faithful assistant.

"Hey Ms. G," Ben returned dully, sounded tired and depressed.

"What's wrong, Ben?" Missy asked, worried. Her loyal sidekick hadn't been quite his normal upbeat self since the death of his cat and she was concerned that he might be slipping into a depression.

"I found out something pretty disturbing tonight," the young man began, haltingly.

"Disturbing?" Missy was really worried now. "What is it, Ben, what happened?"

The young man continued softly, "the lab tests that they did, when, you know..." he trailed off, referring to the death of his cat. "The tests came back and they indicated that it actually was poison that killed Rocky...rat poison."

Missy expressed her horror and sympathy, trying her best to support the emotionally wounded youth, while questions raced through her mind. Rat poison killed Darryl Davis, and now it had killed Ben's cat. Another "mysterious coincidence" that she couldn't ignore. She had seen the large box of rat poison in Andretti's bakery, but he had a solid alibi, so while it seemed more likely that a man with ties to the mob might be responsible for the death of a competitor and an innocent animal, the intelligence that Missy had managed to gather seemed to point to a cranky florist with a sweet tooth. She was more determined than ever to execute her last covert mission under the cover of early morning darkness, and after a virtually sleepless night of tossing and turning, she once again pulled on her yoga pants, paired with a black turtleneck sweater this time, and tucked her blonde curls into a soft black beanie cap. She couldn't allow herself to be discovered by a potentially dangerous human being, and would take every precaution for her safety. Missy felt a bit silly in her all-black garb, but loaded up a bag with a snack, a flashlight, and a first-aid kit (just in case), and headed for her car. She had parked in a remote corner of the parking garage because all of the good spots were taken by the time she arrived home after closing the shop the night before. She played out the strategy of her plan over and over again, trying to prepare for whatever scenario might arise. She was going to park down the block, behind Darryl Davis' house and watch for his daily hydrangea delivery in the pitch dark of pre-dawn. When the mysterious person (whom she now assumed was the Cheesecake lady), delivered the blue blossom, she would maintain a safe distance and follow with her lights off so that she could either verify that it was indeed Strawberry Cheesecake, or not. If the flower deliverer and the Cheesecake lady were one and the same, it didn't seem too far of a stretch (at least in Missy's fevered imagination), to assume that she was the killer. What Missy couldn't figure out was why the unpleasant woman would target her. As far as she knew, she had never met the woman, aside from their encounter in the cupcake shop. She shrugged off her doubts, firmly believing that if she could just provide Chas Beckett with the killer, he'd be able to dig up enough information to prove her guilt, so she set out to do exactly that. So engrossed was she in thinking through the details of her plan, that she failed to notice the dark shadow occupying the back seat of her tiny blue car.

Chapter 16

Tossing her bag in the passenger seat and settling in behind the wheel, Missy didn't even have time to scream as a small but strong hand clamped over her mouth, while a cylinder of cold steel bumped roughly against her temple. Shaking violently, she heard a distinctive click as the gun was cocked, letting her know that her assailant meant business.

"Don't say a word," a voice that sounded vaguely masculine hissed in her ear. "Don't scream, don't even breathe, or you won't live to regret it, Nancy Drew," the somewhat lispy voice warned her mockingly. Missy's heart pounded in her chest. She'd never had any experience with violence or criminals and was at a complete loss as to what to do. She instinctively sensed that her best bet for survival was to do as she was told.

"Slowly take your hands off the steering wheel, and put them behind your head," the sinister voice demanded, still holding the gun to her temple. Missy complied, curbing the impulse to try to knock the gun out of the attacker's hand. "Don't move," the intruder instructed, and Missy heard the familiar rasping sound of duct tape being pulled from a roll. The assailant brought her wrists together roughly and wrapped tape around and between them, even covering her hands, palms together, in layers of the strong, sticky tape. Silent tears slipped down Missy's face, she'd never been more afraid in her entire life. After blindfolding the terrified woman, stuffing a washcloth in her mouth and securing it with more duct tape, the attacker ordered Missy to move to the passenger seat, and then forced her down into the footwell, where she was instructed to stay. The attacker then climbed into the driver's seat, placed a cloth briefly over Missy's nose, causing her to faint and stay in a drugged slumber. Missy's last thought as she drifted into unconsciousness was that she hoped she would live to see another day.

Missy's head throbbed miserably. The washcloth had been removed from her mouth at some point, but her throat was so dry that it might as well have been left in place. She tried weakly to swallow and her tongue stuck to the roof of her mouth at the effort. She was still blindfolded, and even turning her head to the side caused her to feel as though the entire room was rocking, so she stayed as still as possible, listening as intently as her fuzzy head would allow, to try and determine where she was and if she was alone. She was lying on some sort of cold, hard surface, and seemed to be restrained by straps criss-crossing her body. Her hands were still taped together, and her ankles had been secured as well. She attempted to swallow again, wincing at the pain in her throat.

"Trust me honey, this will be much better for you if you just go back to sleep," an effeminate voice dripping with contempt drawled from a bit of a distance. Missy heard the scrape of a chair being pulled back and footsteps moving toward her.

"Thirsty?" the stranger laughed darkly before splashing a vile liquid into Missy's unsuspecting mouth. The moonshine burned, and startled, Missy swallowed reflexively, leading to a hoarse spasm of coughing which burned her lungs and seared her throat. The tears began anew as she sputtered against the harshness of the alcohol, wondering how long this crazed stranger would let her live.

"Who are you? Why are you doing this?" Missy croaked, feeling that she had nothing to lose at this point.

The kidnapper chuckled, an eerie sound that chilled Missy to the bone. Her body was wracked with another bout of shaking as she tried to engage her attacker. "I could ask you the same," the stranger snarled in response. "Everything would have worked out just fine if you hadn't been quite so good at sticking your nose where it didn't belong, Little Miss Cupcakes," the attacker sneered. Missy tried hard to focus on the voice, but she couldn't place it, couldn't even tell whether the person was male or female. She had been quite sure last night that the killer was Strawberry Cheesecake, but now her confidence was rattled. She had no idea how long she'd been unconscious, and wondered if Ben had noticed that she was missing yet. It could take a while, because she often ran errands in the morning while Ben ran the shop. She didn't know if it was even still morning, or the same day. The potential hopelessness of her situation struck her profoundly and her tears flowed freely, despite her dehydration.

"Crying will get you nowhere," the merciless, disembodied voice assured her. "You can cry, scream, throw a tantrum, it doesn't matter. No one can hear you, and more importantly, no one cares," her tormentor taunted. Missy's stomach rolled at the sheer ugliness in both the statement and the tone, but she couldn't allow herself the indulgence of self-pity, she had to think, and fast, of a plan to escape her current predicament.

"I managed to totally elude those bumbling idiots at the police department after I took care of your sister, and they didn't have a clue as to who offed dearest Darryl and your sappy assistant's stupid animal," the kidnapper bragged, much to Missy's horror. The reference to her sister made a fierce nausea, coupled with a murderous rage, rise up within her, but she suffered in silence, still unable to even turn her head. "But no, you and Detective "Prince Charming" were getting way too close. You could've saved yourself if you had just left well enough alone, and gone back to baking your cupcakes, but you just had to be nosy," the assailant groused, escalating Missy's fear. She didn't trust herself to speak, and even if she had - she didn't know what to say, fearing that the slightest remark could send this clearly unbalanced individual over the edge. Apparently the attacker had been partaking of the moonshine that they had tried to foist upon an unsuspecting Missy, and the harsh words were becoming a bit slurred. A tongue obviously loosened by the strong drink seemed to be more than willing to divulge events that had been long kept secrets.

"I loved him," the voice half-sobbed. "I loved that man for years and he wouldn't give me the time of day. He kissed me once you know...I'll never forget it," the killer reminisced. Missy thought that the words would make sense coming from Strawberry Cheesecake, if it was indeed her holding Missy captive, but the more the attacker drank and talked, the less it sounded like the obsessed florist. The timbre of the voice seemed to deepen a bit, and Missy didn't remember Strawberry Cheesecake as having a slight lisp. Still, she couldn't be sure. She was saved the misery of having to listen to any more of the killer's musings when a slightly damp cloth was placed to her nostrils yet again, and the world mercifully went black.

Melissa Gladstone was alone in a place of complete darkness; all day long she twitched and flailed while battling the demons of her dreams. Dragons slain became surging hordes of monsters, human and inhuman. She had accepted her defeat and her body thrummed with the drum beats that signaled her doom as suddenly she was ripped from her slumber. She awoke, still groggy, with a worse headache than before, to the sound of an insistent pounding. The sound made her head tighten as though it was encased in a vise and she wished that whatever was causing the pounding would stop. Through the residual haze of having been drugged, she heard what sounded like Detective Beckett's voice and concluded that she must be dreaming.

"Ms. Gladstone, are you in there?" she heard Chas say, as though from far, far away. She smiled at the sound of his voice, glad that her dreams had suddenly become much more pleasant. "Missy! Talk to me!" the handsome detective demanded, concern coloring his words. The fog that held Missy's mind in its grip parted just then, and she realized that she wasn't dreaming anymore. The pounding became louder, and Chas' voice was real. She tried to respond, but couldn't manage to croak out a response past the dryness in her throat. She tried again and again, but couldn't call out. Just as she began to cry in frustration, she heard an ear-shattering splintering that sounded like a tree had been felled, and suddenly there were voices and sounds filling the room in which she had been kept.

"Missy, are you okay?" she nearly fainted with relief at hearing the detective's voice. She wasn't going to die. Chas was here and he would rescue her. She tried to respond and couldn't.

"Hang on," he encouraged her. "I'm going to get you loosed from all of this tape and we'll get you taken care of." She heard him whisper something about an ambulance to someone nearby, as he cut away the multiple straps binding her to the hard slab on which she rested. Taking off her blindfold, he helped her gently to a sitting position. As Missy's blurred eyes slowly adjusted to being uncovered and adapted to the lights blazing in the room, she saw what seemed to be dozens of police officers and detectives swarming through what looked like a ramshackle cabin. The front door had been utterly destroyed by a battering ram, and she shivered at the chill air seeping in through the remaining slivers of the door. A blanket was wrapped around her shoulders, but didn't quell the tremors that shook her from head to toe. Quickly, but gingerly, Chas worked a field knife through the layers of tape that bound Missy's ankles, wrists and hands, rubbing the affected limbs to increase circulation. A uniformed officer uncapped a bottle of water and held it lightly to Missy's lips, so that she could drink. She felt remarkably better after just a few sips and was able to speak again, though still trembling with shock.

"Where am I? What happened?" she murmured, confused.

"We'll go over all of that in a bit," Beckett promised, still working on removing the copious amounts of tape that the killer had used. Missy nodded, too weak to protest. Things got a bit fuzzy after that, and Missy was vaguely aware of being placed on a gurney and feeling a cold blast of air as she was spirited out of the cabin and into the ambulance that waited, lights flashing.

Chapter 17

Missy awoke, afraid to turn her head or open her eyes, fearing that a debilitating headache would strike yet again. She needn't have worried, however, after a full night's sleep and several bags of intravenous fluid, she was feeling much more like herself when she at last, courageously, slowly opened her eyes.

Looking to her left, she immediately saw Detective Beckett sprawled gracefully in an uncomfortable-looking mauve-colored hospital chair. He was studying her intently, and as soon as she met his gaze, he smiled softly.

"You've had quite a night, Ms. Gladstone," he observed quietly. Missy just smiled ruefully, indicating her agreement. Chas picked up a cup of ice water and held the straw to her lips. Drinking deeply, the water felt amazing on her still-parched throat.

"Thank you," Missy reached up and took the cup of water gratefully. "Now that I'm not woozy from whatever drugs that psycho used on me, tell me what happened," she ordered, continually sipping her water.

"Well, as you might have suspected, we stumbled upon the person who murdered Darryl Davis, and…" the detective frowned slightly, leaving his sentence unfinished.

"...And my sister?" Missy supplied, closing her eyes at the thought.

"Yes," Beckett confirmed.

"Who was it? Was I right, was it that terrible woman from the flower shop?"

she demanded, tears slipping slowly down her cheeks. Chas reached out to brush her tears away lightly with his fingertips.

"No, it wasn't Amanda Madison. She owns the Fleur de Lis, but it wasn't her, it was her assistant, Armand Thibedeaux. Apparently he had dated Darryl Davis briefly, prior to Darryl meeting and becoming infatuated by your sister. He tried and tried to rekindle an interest in Darryl, but Darryl was so fixated on Sherilyn that he had eyes for no one else. Even after your sister rejected him again and again, Darryl refused to go out with Armand. We found information in his cabin that indicated he had plotted your death years ago, as a result of the recipe incident. Armand was fiercely protective of Darryl for some reason, and anyone who could be perceived as a threat to him was targeted for destruction."

"Why did you take my lipstick?" Missy asked, suddenly remembering.

Chas sighed and shook his head. "You knew you were a person of interest. When the lab results came back from the cigarette butt that you provided me, there were trace indications of lipstick. No DNA, just lipstick, so I wanted to do a cross-check that would hopefully rule out the possibility that it was yours," he admitted, shrugging apologetically.

"Well it doesn't take much detective work to determine that," Missy scoffed, "Charles Beckett, you know I don't smoke!"

"That's what you had told me, yes, but I had to be certain."

"So whose lipstick was on that cigarette butt?" Missy was mystified.

"We didn't find out until later. It seems that Armand had a willing accomplice," Chas began.

"What? Who?" Missy interrupted, sitting up straighter in the bed.

"Darryl's sister, Rhonda," the detective replied, shaking his head.

"But...why? Why would his own sister participate in his murder?" Missy was astounded.

Beckett grimaced, dreading the prospect of what he had to tell her next. "She didn't help Armand murder Darryl, she helped him murder Sherilyn. The boy that Rhonda loved when she and Sherilyn were in high school committed suicide when Sherilyn refused to go to the prom with him and Rhonda never got over it. She also was next in line to inherit Darryl's Donuts if something happened to Darryl, despite never having worked in her life, so even though she was unwilling to participate directly, she knew of Armand's plans to murder Darryl and went along with them."

"So why was she lurking around my house at night?" Missy wondered. "That doesn't make sense." She shook her head trying to take it all in.

"You loved Sherilyn, you raised Sherilyn, and you had the successful life, against all odds, that Rhonda had always longed for but didn't know how to achieve. She figured that if you were murdered, it would seem as though the murders were related to the food industry or local business owners rather than personal vendettas, so she volunteered to take you out on Armand's behalf. She'd own Darryl's Donuts, she would have vengeance for lost love, and no one would be the wiser, but you were beginning to figure things out, so Armand kidnapped you himself to speed up the process."

Missy sipped her water, stunned. "So...how did you find me?"

"Your neighbor let us in to your house when we realized you had gone missing, and I found the notebook that you've been keeping. I read about the Cheesecake lady and the hydrangeas and decided to dig deeper. Amanda told me all about the huge crush that Armand had on Darryl, and I got a warrant to search his apartment. While I was there, gathering evidence that linked him to Darryl's murder, I received a call from the state police that Armand had wrapped his car around a tree just a few miles from the cabin that he had inherited from his grandmother a few years ago. He was conscious enough to question and admitted that you were being held captive in the cabin. You pretty much know the rest from there."

"So he's going to jail?" Missy queried, eyes round with fear, remembering her harrowing ordeal.

"He and Rhonda are both going to jail for a very long time," he assured her. "You have nothing more to worry about," he patted her hand gently and smiled.

"You just focus on your recovery and let me worry about the bad guys okay?" Missy smiled in response, nodding. "Good - because when you get out of here, I'm guessing you're going to be hungry for a nice juicy steak." For the first time since she had known him, Chas grinned broadly, and she was filled with hope.

A letter from the Author

To each and every one of my beautiful readers: *I hope you enjoyed this story as much as I enjoyed writing it. Let me what you think by leaving a review!*
I'll be releasing another installment in Late February 2015 so to stay in the loop (and to get free books and other fancy stuff) Join my Book club.

Stay Curious,
Carol Durand

Made in the USA
San Bernardino, CA
12 December 2015